# Two Hoots
# and the Big Bad Bird

by Helen Cresswell
illustrated by Martine Blanc

Crown Publishers, Inc., New York

First published in the United States in 1978
Copyright © 1975 by Ernest Benn Limited
ISBN: 0-517-53281-6

Big Hoot and Little Hoot
live in the woods.
They are not wise.
They are silly.

They fly in the woods
during the day.
Wise owls sleep during
the day and fly
in the woods at night.

One day Little Hoot
saw something in a tree.
"What is that?" he said.
"It is all red."
"I don't know," said Big Hoot.
"But we must be brave.
Let's go look."

They flew to a tree.
"What is it?"
said Little Hoot.
"A bird," said Big Hoot.
"It is a big red bird."

"It is a big bad bird,"
  said Little Hoot.
"Look at it.
  Look at how red it is.
  Look at how big it is.
  I don't like it. Do you?"
"No," said Big Hoot.
"I don't like it at all."

"It will eat us up,"
said Little Hoot.
"No it won't,"
said Big Hoot.
"It is sleeping."

"We must leave,"
said Big Hoot.
"We must tell all
of the wise owls
about the big bad bird.
If we don't, it will
eat us all up."

They flew away.
All of the wise owls
were sleeping.

Big Hoot and Little Hoot
woke them up.
"There is a big bad bird
in the woods," they shouted.
"It will eat us up
if we don't look out."

The wise owls were scared.
"What should we do?"
they cried.
"What should we do?"

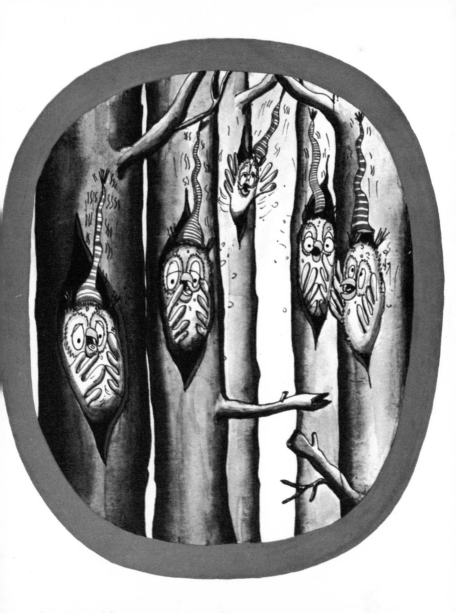

"I don't know,"
  said Big Hoot.
"We are not wise.
  We are silly.
  You decide."
"We must be brave,"
  said the wise owls.
"We must go look at it."

"We will be brave too,"
said Big Hoot.
"We will take you
to the big bad bird."
They flew to a tree.

"It is not there,"
said Big Hoot.
"It must be flying
in the woods."
"It will eat us all up,"
said the wise owls.
"We must hide."
And they all flew away.
They all think there is
a big bad bird in the woods.
But there isn't, is there?
You know what it is,
don't you?

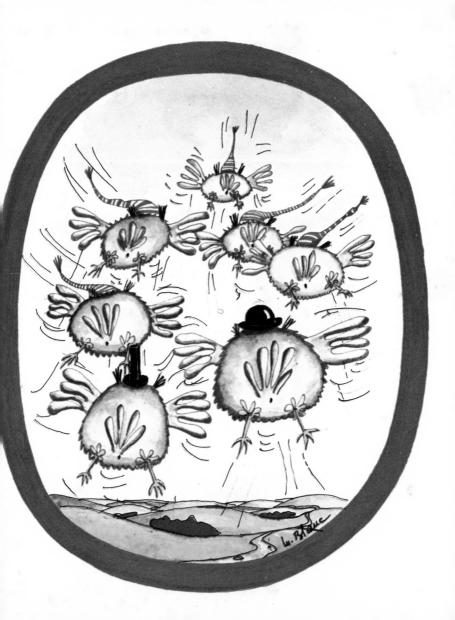

# OTHER EARLY READERS

Two Hoots

Two Hoots Go to the Sea

Two Hoots and the Big Bad Bird

Two Hoots Play Hide-and-Seek